The Ghost
of
Gratiot Road

Here's what readers from around the country are saying about Johnathan Rand's AMERICAN CHILLERS:

"I LOVE your books! They are AWESOME! You are my favorite author."
-Michael M., age 9, Connecticut

"My favorite book so far is Poisonous Pythons Paralyze Pennsylvania. I like your books and hope to read more."
-Jack A., age 8, Michigan

"Hey! If I write something cool about your books, will you put it in that blurb section you have in the front? Because your books really rock!"
-Aarron J., age 10, Ohio

"I never used to like to read, and then I found your books. I've read every single one you've written. I can't stop!"
-Whitney A., age 10, Montana

"I've read all your books, and they scare the daylights out of me!"
-Logan L., age 7, Michigan

"Last summer, we drove to Michigan just so we could visit Chillermania! That place is cool!"
-David L., age 10, Illinois

"My favorite book is Terrifying Toys of Tennessee. That book is terrifying, just like the title says!"
-Allison H., age 13, Iowa

"YOUR BOOKS ARE AWESOME! I have already read 33 of your books and starting the 34th."
                    -Dante J., age 8, Pennsylvania

"I just wanted to let you know that we read WICKED VELOCIRAPTORS OF WEST VIRGINIA in our class, and everyone loved it! I can't wait to read more of your books!"
                    -Corbin S., age 10, West Virginia

"How come your books are the freakiest in the world? I've never read any other books like them. Keep writing!"
                    -Erik R., age 11, Delaware

"I got one of your books for my birthday, and I loved it. Now, I can't stop reading them!"
                    -Samantha P., age 11, Michigan

"I don't know if you know this, but everyone at our school is hooked on CHILLERS! They're the only books we read!"
                    -Marcus B., age 10, Ohio

"You came to our school last year, and it was the BEST assembly we ever had! Please come back!"
                    -Tyler S., age 9, California

"We had a contest at school to see who could read the most books written by you. I won! I've read every single book you've ever written. I love all of them! My favorite is WISCONSIN WEREWOLVES, because that's were I live. That book creeped me out really bad. It's great!"
                    -Addison S., age 12, Wisconsin

"After reading DANGEROUS DOLLS OF DELAWARE, I had to sleep with the light on for two weeks. I can't believe how much that book freaked me out!"

-Rick A., age 11, Alabama

"I know your books aren't real, but when I'm reading them, it seems like they are. How do you do that?"

-Missy G., age 10, Oklahoma

"I love all of your books, but I have one suggestion: write faster!"

-Sean J., age 8, North Carolina

"When you write, do you wear those weird glasses? If you do, don't ever take them off, because your books are super awesome!"

-James T., age 10, Rhode Island

"I've read a lot of books, but yours are the best in the world! I think I've read all of them at least twice, and I read MUTANTS MAMMOTHS OF MONTANA three times! It's my all-time favorite book!"

-Melissa G, age 12, Michigan

"I got all three Adventure Club books for my birthday, and they're the best! Write more Adventure Club stories!"

-Namute H., age 11, Indiana

Got something cool to say about Johnathan Rand's books? Let us know, and we might publish it right here! Send your short blurb to:

Chiller Blurbs
281 Cool Blurbs Ave.
Topinabee, MI 49791

Don't miss these exciting, action-packed books by Johnathan Rand:

Michigan Chillers:

#1: Mayhem on Mackinac Island
#2: Terror Stalks Traverse City
#3: Poltergeists of Petoskey
#4: Aliens Attack Alpena
#5: Gargoyles of Gaylord
#6: Strange Spirits of St. Ignace
#7: Kreepy Klowns of Kalamazoo
#8: Dinosaurs Destroy Detroit
#9: Sinister Spiders of Saginaw
#10: Mackinaw City Mummies
#11: Great Lakes Ghost Ship
#12: AuSable Alligators
#13: Gruesome Ghouls of Grand Rapids
#14: Bionic Bats of Bay City

American Chillers:

#1: The Michigan Mega-Monsters
#2: Ogres of Ohio
#3: Florida Fog Phantoms
#4: New York Ninjas
#5: Terrible Tractors of Texas
#6: Invisible Iguanas of Illinois
#7: Wisconsin Werewolves
#8: Minnesota Mall Mannequins
#9: Iron Insects Invade Indiana
#10: Missouri Madhouse
#11: Poisonous Pythons Paralyze Pennsylvania
#12: Dangerous Dolls of Delaware
#13: Virtual Vampires of Vermont
#14: Creepy Condors of California
#15: Nebraska Nightcrawlers
#16: Alien Androids Assault Arizona
#17: South Carolina Sea Creatures
#18: Washington Wax Museum
#19: North Dakota Night Dragons
#20: Mutant Mammoths of Montana
#21: Terrifying Toys of Tennessee
#22: Nuclear Jellyfish of New Jersey
#23: Wicked Velociraptors of West Virginia
#24: Haunting in New Hampshire
#25: Mississippi Megalodon

Freddie Fernortner, Fearless First Grader:

#1: The Fantastic Flying Bicycle
#2: The Super-Scary Night Thingy
#3: A Haunting We Will Go
#4: Freddie's Dog Walking Service
#5: The Big Box Fort
#6: Mr. Chewy's Big Adventure
#7: The Magical Wading Pool
#8: Chipper's Crazy Carnival

Adventure Club series:

#1: Ghost in the Graveyard
#2: Ghost in the Grand
#3: The Haunted Schoolhouse

For Teens:

PANDEMIA: A novel of the bird flu and the end of the world
(written with Christopher Knight)

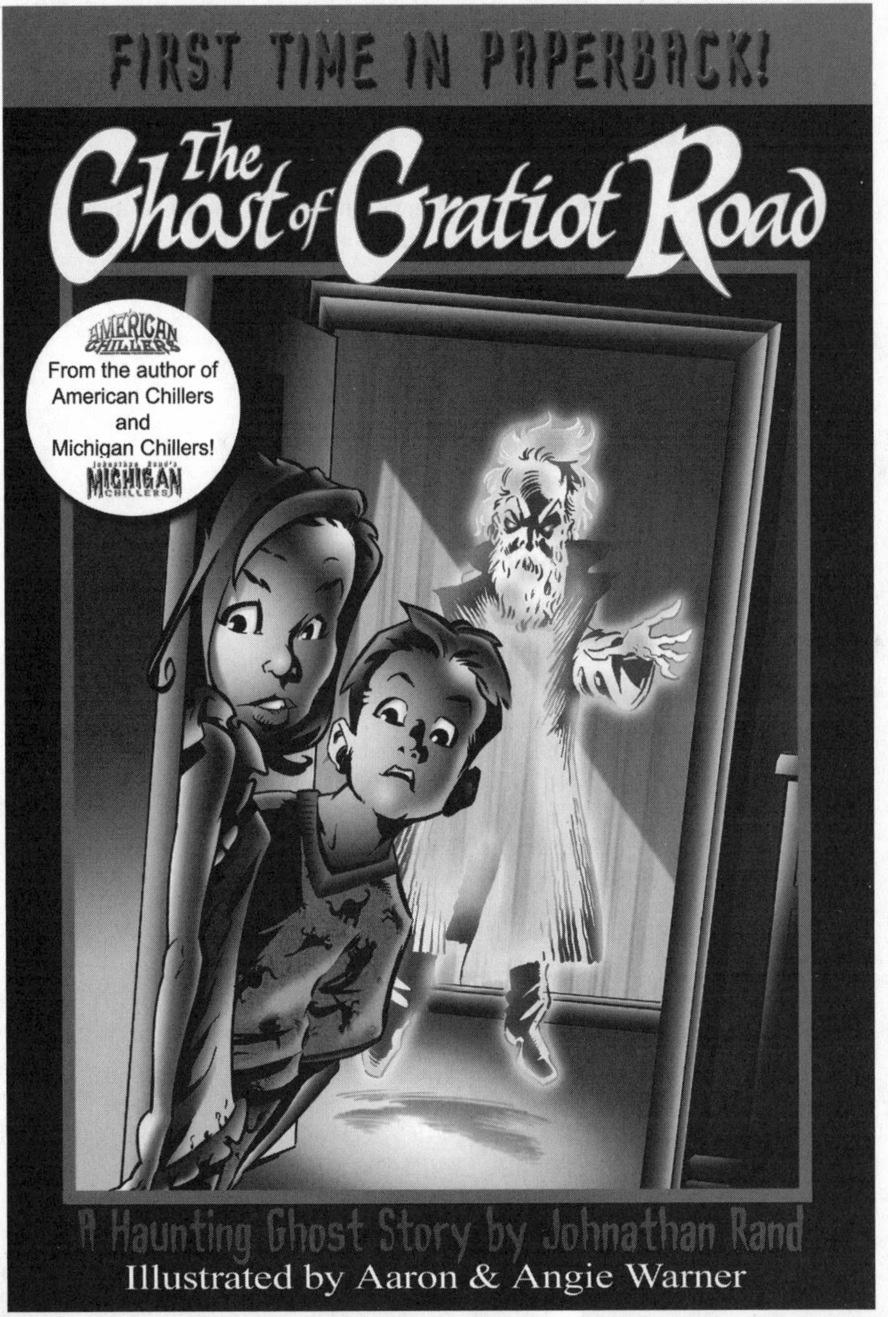

FIRST TIME IN PAPERBACK!
The Ghost of Gratiot Road
AMERICAN CHILLERS
From the author of
American Chillers
and
Michigan Chillers!
MICHIGAN CHILLERS
A Haunting Ghost Story by Johnathan Rand
Illustrated by Aaron & Angie Warner

An AudioCraft Publishing, Inc. book

Book storage and warehouses provided by Chillermania!©
Indian River, Michigan

Warehouse security provided by:
Lily Munster, Scooby-Boo, & Spooky Dude

The Ghost of Gratiot Road
ISBN 13-digit: 978-1-893699-98-4

Librarians/Media Specialists:
PCIP/MARC records available **free of charge** at
www.americanchillers.com

Cover and interior illustrations by
Aaron & Angie Warner, © 2007 AudioCraft Publishing, Inc.
Cover layout by Sue Harring

The Ghost
of
Gratiot Road

VISIT CHILLERMANIA!

WORLD HEADQUARTERS FOR BOOKS BY JOHNATHAN RAND!

Yooperland

Indian River

Alpena

Traverse City

MICHIGAN

CHILLERMANIA!

I-75 Exit 313 then south 1 mile!

Mt. Pleasant

Bay City

Grand Rapids

Lansing

Kalamazoo

Detroit

Visit the HOME for books by Johnathan Rand! Featuring books, hats, shirts, bookmarks and other cool stuff not available anywhere else in the world! Plus, watch the American Chillers website for news of special events and signings at *CHILLERMANIA!* with author Johnathan Rand! Located in northern lower Michigan, on I-75! Take exit 313 . . . then south 1 mile! For more info, call (231) 238-0338. And be afraid! Be veeeery afraaaaaaiiiid . . . .

chapter one

1

The sun was just beginning to rise as my mom called out from the kitchen.

"Okay, you guys! Time to get up! It's going to be a busy day!"

I'd been awake for awhile already, waiting. I was excited . . . and a little nervous. We'd arrived at our new house late last night. After searching for a home for almost a year, Mom and Dad found one: in Saginaw on Gratiot Road, about two hours away from our home in Muskegon. We'd looked in a bunch of cities, too: Holland, Port Huron, Harbor Springs,

Traverse City, Alpena, even Marquette—which is way up in Michigan's Upper Peninsula. Finally, we found a home that was perfect.

Almost everything we owned was still in a big, rented truck parked in the driveway. The only thing in my new bedroom was the bed and a small suitcase with a single change of clothes. All of my other things: my dresser, clothing, stereo—everything—were still packed away in the truck.

In the bedroom next to mine, I could hear my brothers arguing. Brandon is eleven, one year younger than me, and Davis is five. They usually get along pretty well, but this morning, Davis was mad at Brandon for stepping on his toy truck. Davis found it in the attic of our old home last year, in one of the boxes that had been left by the previous owner of the house. The truck was old and handmade, and, although it was pretty beat up, Davis loved it. It was his favorite toy.

I ignored the commotion, got up and got dressed, and went downstairs.

"Ready to unload and unpack, Kirsten?" Mom asked me. There were three bowls on the kitchen counter, and she was pouring cereal.

I nodded and smiled. "I've been waiting for this day for a month!" I exclaimed. "I'm going to miss my friends, but I'll make new ones here. And our new house is cool!"

"This isn't a new house," Brandon said as he came down the stairs. He has dark brown hair, and it was all messy from sleeping. "It's an old one, just like our other place."

"But this place is bigger," Mom said, "and your father will have a big office upstairs. Now that he's started his own business, he can work from home. We won't have to move again."

I was looking forward to that. It seemed like every year we had to move, because the company Dad worked for constantly transferred him to different cities in Michigan. Hopefully, this would be the last time we moved.

It took us most of the day to unload and unpack. Of course, Davis was too little to help, so he just played with his truck in the yard while we did all the hard work. Finally, just as the sun was going down, we finished. There was still a little unpacking to do, but that could wait until the next day. Right now, we were tired and hungry. Dad called to have a pizza delivered, which was great. Pizza is my favorite food in the whole world!

Later, as I was getting ready for bed, Brandon came to my bedroom door.

"Hey, Kirsten," he said. "Did you notice anything strange about this place?"

I thought about it for a moment. "No," I replied, shaking my head. "Not really. Why?"

Brandon looked around. "I don't know," he said. "But it *is* an old house. I just wonder if there are any ghosts here."

I frowned. "Don't be silly," I said. "There are no ghosts here. Ghosts aren't real."

"They might be," he said, looking around as if he might see a ghost that very moment.

"Well, I'm not afraid of any ghosts," I said. And I wasn't. I don't believe that ghosts exist.

That is, I *didn't*. Not at the time.

Now, however, I know better.

Brandon and Davis went to bed in their room. They have a bunk bed, and Davis sleeps on the bottom bunk. Mom or Dad usually check on us before we go to sleep. Maybe one of them did. I didn't know, because I fell asleep the moment my head hit the pillow. All that unpacking really tired me out!

Later that night, I awoke. Moonlight streamed through the window, and I was confused, not knowing where I was. It took a moment to realize I was in my new bedroom, in our new home, in Saginaw. My bedside clock glowed. It was just after three in the morning. My window was open a little bit, and I could hear crickets chirping. Somewhere, far off, a car horn honked.

Suddenly, I realized there was a dark figure standing by my window. At first, I thought it was the shadow of a shrub.

Then, I realized it wasn't a shadow at all. Someone—or some*thing*—was standing in front of my window!

chapter two

I opened my mouth to scream . . . but nothing came out! All I could do was make a strange, wheezing sound. No matter how hard I tried, I couldn't scream. It was like all my breath had been taken away.

Then . . . the shadow vanished. It just disappeared . . . like it had never been there at all!

I froze. I was terrified, and every muscle in my body tensed. Then, after a moment, I pulled the covers up to my chin. All the while, I never took my eyes off the window.

What was that? I wondered. *Was someone really standing there . . . or was it just my imagination?* I've done that before. Once, I woke up in the middle of the night and was *sure* I saw the face of a dog at my window. I screamed like crazy! Mom and Dad came running in, and we discovered that it wasn't a dog at all . . . it was only the shadow of some tree branches. Boy, did I ever feel silly! But, at the time, it really *did* look like a dog . . . and a big one, too. It was pretty freaky.

Maybe that's all it was this time: the shadow of tree branches. And the more I waited and thought about it, the more I convinced myself it was nothing. I hadn't seen anything, I was sure. It had only been my imagination. I wasn't scared, and I would prove it . . . by getting up and getting a glass of water.

I stood and stretched. Cool night air drifted through my open bedroom window. I walked out of my bedroom and strode into the hall. A night light glowed near the floor: the same night light we'd had at our old home in Muskegon. I wandered down the hall to the kitchen, where Mom had left the stove light on . . . just like she had at our old home. On the refrigerator were dozens of magnets, each one a different letter of the alphabet. Mom and Dad gave me them for my birthday a couple of years ago, and we all had fun making up poems and sentences. The magnets were some of the first things to be unpacked. It was nice to know that some of the things in our old home were now a part of our new home.

In the kitchen, I found a glass and filled it under the faucet. After taking a few sips, I placed it on the counter. I felt better, and I was glad I hadn't screamed in my room. That would have brought Mom and Dad running, just like the time I thought I saw the dog at the window.

I was still thirsty, so I picked up the glass and sipped again. I began thinking about our new home. It was great that Dad was going to be able to work out of our house. He does something with computers, and he works with big companies all over the state . . . which was why he traveled so much. But now he would be working in our house, which meant we would see him a lot more. He said that now he would be able to go to my soccer games, once I joined the local team. He missed most of my games in Muskegon because he was traveling.

Then, I thought about Brandon talking about ghosts in our new home. Brandon has always been a scaredy-cat, but I never thought he would believe in ghosts. He had really seemed frightened. Sure, our new home was old . . . but so was our home in Muskegon. But Brandon has always had an imagination that gets away from him. He's always been really good at coming up with stories . . . especially if he is in trouble. Once, he tried to convince his teacher that a giant baboon took his homework! He said the baboon escaped from the zoo, and that he was on the loose and very dangerous. As you might have guessed, his teacher didn't believe one word of it.

I finished sipping and returned the glass to the counter . . . and that's when I heard a noise.

A creaking sound, like an old board being stepped on.

A shiver trickled down my back. My skin suddenly felt tingly and clammy. I strained to hear more, but the only sound was the thin, steady hum of the refrigerator a few feet away.

After a moment, when I didn't hear anything more, I figured that it was just the old house settling. Our old house sometimes did that. Dad said that houses will continue to settle for years and years after they're built, and that's what causes the noises. When wood shifts even a tiny bit, it can create squeaks and creaks as it moves against other wood.

I left the kitchen. Just as I was about to turn and go down the hall, I heard the noise again. Once more, a shiver snaked along my spine. I turned slowly, looking into the gloomy living room. It was dark, but bluish-white moonlight was streaming through the window. I could see the shape of our couch and Dad's recliner.

Suddenly, a dark figure moved out from the shadows . . . and I could clearly see the silhouette of someone standing in the living room!

I drew in a deep breath, determined to let out the shrillest scream I could muster. My gasp must have been loud: so loud, in fact, that it scared whoever was in the living room! And just as I was about to run down the hall and wake up Mom and Dad, I heard a voice.

"Kirsten? Is that you?"

It was Brandon!

Now, I was *mad*. I don't know what he was doing in the living room, but he'd really scared me.

"What are *you* doing up?!?!" I hissed. "It's after three o'clock in the morning!"

"I was sleepwalking again," he replied in a thick whisper. "You woke me up and freaked me out."

Now, I know that might sound unbelievable to you, but Brandon probably wasn't making it up. He *does* have a habit of sleepwalking. He started doing it a couple of years ago. He'll walk all around the house, in the middle of the night, while he's asleep! That's really weird, but I guess there are a lot of people who do the same thing.

Strange. But, then again, I've always thought my brother was weird.

Brandon went to the kitchen to get a drink of water, and I went back to bed. He sure had startled me, and I wondered if he would keep sleepwalking as he grew older. I didn't wonder for too long, though, because I slept through the rest of the night.

The next day was sunny and warm. It was June, and we had the whole summer ahead of us, since school wouldn't start up until September. I like school, and I was looking forward to meeting new friends. But right now, I was excited to have the summer off! We had a new house, and there were lots of things to explore around our neighborhood, including our yard. It was big—a lot bigger than our yard in Muskegon—and it had lots of different kinds of trees: white pines, red pines, maples, oaks, and a gigantic willow tree in front, near the sidewalk. Its branches hung down like wires, and the slightest breeze caused the leaves to tremble and sway.

Dad left to head to Muskegon that morning. He had to drive there with a truck to pick up a few things that didn't fit in the truck on our first trip. He wouldn't be getting home until the next day. He said that when he got back, we were going to have a barbecue in the backyard. That would be fun!

Brandon and I spent the whole day traipsing around the yard, and we kept an eye on Davis, who spent most of his time in the sandbox with his toy truck or playing on an old swing set left by the previous owners of the house. There were other homes in the distance, but we couldn't see most of them because of the trees. At our old home, all of the houses had been tightly nestled together on the block, and there weren't nearly as many trees. Here, at our new home on Gratiot Road, the houses were much farther apart, and there were lots of large fields. For me, it was *perfect*.

"I'm going to go inside and grab some lunch," Brandon said. "You want anything?"

It was almost noon, but I'd had a big breakfast and wasn't hungry. "No," I said. "I'll stay out here and keep an eye on Davis." Brandon bounded off without another word, skipped up the front steps, and vanished into the house.

I stood in the bright sun, staring up. Our new home was really cool looking. The house was white and had been freshly-painted. All the windows had red shutters, which looked kind of cool. Most homes don't have shutters anymore. It was old, sure—but it was big, and it looked a little creepy. The windows on the second floor were like eyes, and they all seemed to be staring at me.

Then, I remembered being scared the night before, in my bedroom, when I thought I'd seen a face at my window. It was silly, I know.

But—

What if I *hadn't* imagined it? What if—

I turned around to check on Davis. He was puttering around in the sandbox, pushing his truck around and making engine noises. So, I turned and looked at my bedroom window. There were a couple of shrubs around it, but I wondered how I could have imagined seeing something that looked like a face.

I walked toward the house, toward my bedroom window. There really didn't appear to be any branches nearby that could have cast a shadow that looked like a face, and I began to wonder: *Had there been someone at my window?*

On the ground, I received my answer. There was a folded piece of paper laying in the grass, next to a dark green shrub.

When I knelt down to look closer, I gasped. My skin grew cold, even in the warm sunshine. The hair on the back of my neck felt electrified.

The note was addressed to me! Someone had written my name on the note!

That alone was horrifying. But when I read what the letter said, I thought I was going to die of fright!

chapter four

I trembled as I unfolded the note and read the words.

Dear Kirsten:

My name is Mortimer Feinburg, and I am a ghost. You and your family have intruded in my home on Gratiot Road. If you do not leave right away, I will continue to haunt you and your family. I will make living here very difficult for all of you! YOU HAVE BEEN WARNED!

Signed,

Mortimer Feinburg

By the time I finished reading the note, I was trembling so badly I nearly dropped the paper! *A ghost?!?! Living in our new home?!?!*

I was horrified. Brandon and I had been talking about ghosts just yesterday. And, I had spotted a face at my window last night! Now, I knew the truth: there really was a ghost in our home, and he wanted us out!

I ran into the house, carrying the letter.

"Mom!" I shouted as the screen door banged shut behind me. I sprinted across the wood floor, through the living room, where I almost ran into Brandon. He was carrying half a sandwich, and he leapt to get out of my way.

"Man, what's up with *you?*" he asked.

I ignored him and raced into the kitchen. "Mom!" I shouted. "There's a ghost in our house!"

Mom was unpacking a box of dishes. She turned to me and frowned.

"A ghost, huh?" she smirked.

"No, really!" I exclaimed. I held out the paper

for her to see. "Look!"

"Where is Davis?" she asked. "You're supposed to be watching him."

I glanced through the kitchen window and pointed. "He's fine," I said. "He's right there, in the sandbox." Mom turned and glanced out the window. Then she took the note and read it, smiling. When she finished, she handed it back to me. "I think one of the new neighborhood kids is up to a prank," she said. "There are no such things as ghosts."

"But I saw someone at my window last night!" I pleaded. "I thought it was a shadow, but it wasn't! It was a ghost!"

"Kirsten," Mom said sternly, "there are no such things as ghosts. You know better."

"But—"

Mom shook her head. "I'm really busy right now," she said, "and I don't want to hear anything more about ghosts. And don't you go telling your brothers that there are ghosts here. They'll be scared out of their minds, especially little Davis."

I sulked away. Maybe Mom was right. Maybe it

was just one of the neighborhood kids playing a joke. I hoped to find out who, because I would be sure to get him or her back.

I crumbled up the note and tossed it into the waste basket. That was the end of that. I wasn't going to be frightened by some kid playing a joke.

Outside, I met up with Brandon and Davis in the backyard. Davis was on the swing, and Brandon was pushing him.

"What's your problem?" Brandon asked. "You almost ran me over in the house."

"Oh, nothing," I replied. I remembered Mom had told me not to say anything to Brandon or Davis, because they might get freaked out by the letter . . . even if it was just neighborhood kids pulling a prank.

But then I had another thought: what if Brandon was the one who wrote the letter?

"Actually," I said, "I have a question for you. Come here." I motioned him to follow me as I turned and walked away. I didn't want Davis to overhear.

Davis protested as Brandon left him alone to swing by himself. "Push! Push!" he wailed.

"In a minute," Brandon said. "I'll be right back."

He approached me. "What?" he asked.

"Did you write a note and put it outside my bedroom window?" I asked.

He frowned. "Why would I do that?" he replied.

"Maybe to try to freak me out," I shot back.

"Kirsten, if I really want to freak you out, the best way is to catch a snake and chase you around the yard."

"Very funny," I sneered. But he was right. I don't particularly care for snakes. Once, he got in trouble for chasing me around the yard with a garter snake he'd caught.

Brandon walked off, returning to the swing set to push Davis. I walked off alone and sat beneath the big willow tree.

Mom is probably right, I thought. *That note was written by some neighborhood kid trying to scare me. Or us. That's all it was.*

Well, as it turned out, the note *wasn't* written by a neighborhood kid. And later that night, after dark, I would come face to face with the author of the letter.

chapter five

I went to bed at eight o'clock. Mom lets me stay up for an extra hour and read, so that's what I did. I'd been reading a really scary book about giant spiders in Saginaw, and it gave me the creeps. Spiders don't really bother me, but these spiders were as big as cars. Sure, the story wasn't true, but it still freaked me out. I wondered where the author came up with all of his weird ideas.

45

By nine o'clock, I was almost finished with the book, but I was really tired. I would finish it in the morning. I put the book on the dresser next to my bed, turned off my reading lamp, and fell asleep.

A creaking sound woke me up. I had no idea what time it was. The only thing I knew for sure was that my bedroom door was opening. I was really frightened, but only for a moment. As soon as I turned on my reading lamp, I saw Brandon standing in the doorway. He was wearing his favorite pajamas: the blue ones with dinosaurs all over.

"What are you doing up?" I asked, glancing at the clock. It was after midnight.

"I think I saw a ghost!" he hissed. His voice trembled, and I could tell that he was really spooked.

"You were just dreaming," I said. "Go back to bed."

"No, really, Kirsten," Brandon said as he pushed the door open farther and came into my room. "I really think I saw one!"

He looked really serious. Oh, I still wondered if he was just making it up, but he really *did* seem freaked out.

"But first," he continued, "let me tell you something: *I* was the one who wrote that letter and put it by your window."

I gasped. *"You?!?! Why?!?!"*

"I was just having fun, playing a joke," he answered.

"But when I asked you about it today, you said you didn't do it," I said angrily. "You fibbed!"

Brandon shook his head. "I never said I didn't. All I said was there were better ways to freak you out. When you saw me sleepwalking last night, I hadn't been sleepwalking at all. I had just come in from planting the letter by your window."

I thought about that for a moment. He was right: he never did tell me that he wasn't the one who wrote the note.

"Anyway," Brandon said, "I wrote the note. After we had talked about ghosts earlier in the day, I thought it would be a great way to scare you. But I think I saw a *real* ghost! You have to believe me!"

I didn't know whether I believed him or not, but

I let him continue.

"I heard a noise in my bedroom," he said. "When I opened my eyes, I saw a faint white thing by my closet, and I realized it was a man. Only . . . it was like he was made of fog or something. When he turned, I could see what he looked like. He had a thick mustache and a beard."

"What happened to him?" I asked.

"He just sort of faded away," Brandon replied.

I frowned at him. I didn't know whether to believe him or not.

"I'm telling you the truth, Kirsten! I tried to scare you with that note, and I'm sorry. But I think there really is a ghost in our house!

It was hard to believe what he was saying. Sure, he had tried to trick me with the letter. But he seemed serious when he spoke of the ghost in his bedroom.

"Is Davis still sleeping?" I asked.

Brandon nodded. "Davis would sleep through an earthquake," he said.

"Well, I still think you were probably just dreaming," I said. "Mom told me today: there's no such thing as ghosts. Go back to bed."

"But what if he comes back?" Brandon said. "What do I do?"

"I don't know," I said. I was getting tired of listening to him. "Tell him to get you a banana milkshake or something. Now, go back to bed before Mom and Dad hear us and we both get into trouble."

Reluctantly, Brandon left. I turned my light off, knowing full well he hadn't seen a ghost. After all: Mom *did* say that there was no such thing as ghosts, and Mom was usually right about everything.

As it turns out, Mom was wrong this time. Brandon was right: he *had* seen a ghost, and soon, all of us would know the truth.

I dozed off, not knowing that a nightmare was about to unfold for my entire family.

chapter six

In the morning, I awoke to gray skies and a fine drizzle falling. I was disappointed, because I wanted to spend more time outside. I had been thinking of hopping on my bike and taking a ride around the neighborhood, but not if it rained all day.

The smells of breakfast teased my nostrils: bacon, eggs, and toast. I got up and went into the kitchen. Brandon and Davis were already up. They were seated at the counter, eating ravenously. Mom was preparing another plate.

"There you are, sleepyhead," Mom said with a smile. She placed the plate on the counter, and steam drifted up from the morsels. "I was just about to come and get you."

As I sat down, Davis burped. Brandon giggled, and Mom frowned. "Davis," she said, "what do you say?"

"Scoose me," Davis replied.

"When will Dad be home?" I asked as I picked up a fork.

"Sometime later this afternoon," Mom replied. "He called and said the truck is all packed, and he'll be on his way soon."

"Are we still having a barbeque tonight?" I asked.

Mom nodded. "That's still the plan," Mom answered. "Unless it keeps drizzling."

And that's what it did. All day, the rain came down. It didn't let up at all, and I wound up staying indoors. I played a couple of games with my brothers.

Davis seemed more interested in pushing his little truck around the house. Brandon played with various toys, but he would get bored with them quickly and move on to something else. He complained to Mom that he couldn't play any computer games because Dad hadn't unpacked and set up the computer yet.

Me? I worked on a jigsaw puzzle, read for a while, then went back to working on the puzzle. I went into the kitchen and used the letter magnets on the refrigerator to spell out 'WELCOME HOME DAD'. He would like that when he got home later that day. Then, I watched television for awhile. Not much was on, and I got bored.

Dad came home in the afternoon. He liked my message on the refrigerator. He said he was glad to be back, and that it was his last trip out of town for a long time. He was looking forward to working out of the house, not having to travel nearly as much. But the real bummer was that we couldn't have a barbeque, because it was still raining out. Mom made hamburgers, but it wasn't the same.

So, for the most part, the day was normal. It

was after we all went to bed when the real crazy things started to happen.

I hadn't talked to Brandon about what he saw in his bedroom the night before, and he didn't bring it up all day. I think he realized that he had probably been dreaming and hadn't seen a ghost, after all. But again, later in the night, I heard a squeak by my door.

Then, it stopped.

I waited . . . then, I heard the sound again. My door was open a tiny crack, and a faint yellow glow from the hall nightlight streamed in.

Brandon is trying to scare me again, I thought. *Well, we'll just see about that!*

Very slowly, I slipped out of bed. I tiptoed on my bare feet across the floor as quietly as I could. On the other side of the bedroom door, Brandon must have moved: I heard two short squeaks, and the door opened another inch.

This is going to be good, I thought. *I'm going to scare him into outer space.*

I approached the door and carefully grabbed the knob. Suddenly, I threw the door open, intending to raise my arms and make a hissing sound—but I didn't have a chance.

What was in front of me, standing in the hallway, wasn't Brandon.

It wasn't Davis, and it wasn't Mom or Dad.

It was the ghost of an old man . . . and let me tell you: he looked *angry*.

chapter seven

The ghost looked just like Brandon had described. He was cloudy and misty-white, but his features were hazy and distorted. Oh, it was definitely a man, or the ghost of a man, for sure. He was the same size as a normal man, and I could see his beard and thick mustache. His hair was a little long, not quite reaching his shoulders. He was wearing an overcoat and boots. But he didn't seem to be standing on the floor. His boots were a few inches off the ground, and he seemed to be floating in the air.

I have never been so scared in my entire life. I couldn't scream; I couldn't move. I couldn't go anywhere, because the ghost was blocking the way!

But if I thought I was scared then, it was *nothing* compared to the horror I felt when the ghost began talking. He was speaking, but he was really hard to understand. He sounded far away, and his words were garbled. As he spoke, he raised his hand toward me, like he was reaching for something.

I saw a motion down the hall, and Brandon appeared. He let out a screech that was so loud he scared me even more. I heard more noises: a commotion from the other end of the hall, in Mom and Dad's room. Then, their door burst open, and Mom shrieked.

Dad came down the hall, walking slowly. "Kirsten," he ordered, "back away. Get into your room. Slowly."

I took a step back, and then another. As I did, the figure of the man became murkier. He became like smoke, swirling and drifting, seeping away, blending into the air. In a few seconds, he was completely gone. I was staring at nothing but thin air.

Dad approached slowly. He waved his hand in the air cautiously, in the very spot where the ghost had been. There was nothing there. The ghost had completely vanished.

"I told you!" Brandon shouted. "That's the dude I saw last night!"

"You saw it last night?" Dad asked. By now, Mom had come rushing down the hall. She ran into my room and hugged me. "Are you all right?" she asked.

"Yeah," I said. "Just scared."

"I saw that thing last night, in my bedroom," Brandon repeated. "I told Kirsten about it."

I nodded. "He did," I said.

"Why didn't you tell your mother?" Dad asked.

"Because Kirsten didn't believe me, and I didn't think Mom would, either. And I wasn't sure that I had actually seen anything. I thought it could have been a dream, like Kirsten told me."

"That was no dream," Dad said. "We all saw it."

"And he was saying something to me," I said. "It sounded like he wanted something, but I can't be sure. But he looked mad about something."

"What are we going to do?" Brandon asked.

Dad paused a moment. "I don't know," he finally said. "I didn't think ghosts were real."

"Maybe we should find a ghost-buster," Brandon offered.

"You know," Mom said, "that's not a bad idea. Maybe we could find one of those people that we see on television."

"You mean a medium?" Dad asked.

I'd heard about mediums; they're supposed to be people who can contact ghosts and spirits. Some of them even say they can get rid of ghosts.

"Yeah," Mom replied. "Maybe, if we could find one, they could tell us what to do."

"Well," Dad said, "we'll figure it out in the morning. Brandon and Kirsten: you two leave your bedroom doors open. If you see that thing again, you holler. Is Davis still sleeping?"

Brandon turned and poked his head into his bedroom. "Like a log," he replied. "Just like always."

So, that's what we did: we all went back to bed. I left my door open, just like Dad had instructed. It was a long time before I was able to fall back to sleep.

When I woke up, the sun was streaming through my window. The rain was gone, and I was excited about getting on my bike and going for a ride around the neighborhood.

I stood, and it was then I remembered the events of the previous night. I dressed quickly and went into the living room. Mom and Dad were sipping coffee, talking. The television was on, but there was no sound. A big telephone book was open on the coffee table.

"We found someone who will come and have a look around," Mom said.

"A medium?" I asked.

"She was listed in the phone book," Dad explained. "She's coming over this morning. She says she'll be able to tell us if there is a ghost here and what we can do about it."

I couldn't believe I was having this conversation with my parents. The day before, they would have laughed if someone told them there were ghosts in our house. But they'd seen it for themselves, so they *had* to believe.

Later that morning, the doorbell rang. I was on the couch, reading, trying to keep my mind on other things besides ghosts. Still, my eyes kept wandering around the room. At any moment, I expected a ghost to appear. None did.

Mom opened the front door. There stood a woman with gray hair and thick glasses. She was tall . . . almost as tall as Dad. She wore a dark brown dress and brown shoes.

But before Mom could say one word or ask her to come inside, a horrified look suddenly came over the woman's face . . . and she began screaming!

chapter eight

The woman was terrified, and she even scared me! I mean, this was supposed to be someone who was familiar with ghosts. What could possibly be in our home to make her so frightened?

In two seconds, I got my answer.

The woman raised her hand and pointed to the outer portion of the doorway.

"A spider!" she exclaimed. "I can't stand them!

Get rid of it!"

A spider? I thought. *She's that freaked out by a silly little spider?* Oh, I don't care for spiders myself . . . but I don't find anything scary about them.

Mom took a step outside the door and looked up. "I don't think he'll hurt you," Mom said. "In fact, he just crawled in between the wood. He's gone now."

That seemed to calm the woman. She put one hand on her chest and let out a deep breath. "I've been terrified by spiders since I was little," she said. "I don't know why. I know that most of them don't bite, but they have always scared me."

All the commotion brought my dad running down the steps.

"What's wrong?" he said as he hurried through the living room to the front door. Brandon and Davis were now there, too. Brandon was holding a model car he had been working on, and Davis was carrying his old wooden truck.

"Everything's fine," Mom replied. "Just a spider, that's all." Then, she spoke to the woman. "You must be Mrs. Withers."

The woman took a few wary steps forward. She glanced up a couple of times to make sure the spider didn't come back. Then, she came into the house.

"Yes, that is me. I'm—"

She stopped speaking in mid-sentence. Her eyes bounced around the room, but her body remained frozen. "Oh, yes," she said, "there's definitely a presence here. Most definitely. I can sense it."

She closed her eyes and breathed in deeply through her nose. I hate to say it, but I thought she was acting a little weird. Then again: what had happened last night had been pretty weird, too.

Davis became bored and walked down the hall to his bedroom. Brandon came over and sat next to me on the couch.

"She's a little strange, huh?" he whispered.

"Yeah, but there's nothing wrong with being a little strange," I whispered back, *"especially if she can get rid of our ghost."*

Mrs. Withers closed her eyes and raised her arms. "Yes, he's here, he's here," she said in an odd, sing-song voice. It was actually sort of creepy.

"Who's *he?*" Dad asked.

"I don't know," Mrs. Withers replied. "Sometimes, all I can feel is energy, like right now." She opened her eyes and lowered her arms. "But you definitely have a ghost here. Please . . . would you mind if I walked through your house alone?"

"That would be fine," Mom said. "Whatever you need."

"Good. That will tell me much more about just what is happening in your home."

And with that, Mrs. Withers drifted off. First, she headed down the hall and went into my room. Then, she went to Brandon and Davis's room. I could hear Davis talking to her.

"You wanna play with my truck?" he asked.

Mrs. Withers laughed. "Not now, little one, not now," she said. "I have work to do."

She came out of the bedroom and back into the living room.

"Where do the stairs go?" she asked, pointing to the other side of the room.

"I have my office up there," Dad replied. "And

there's another room for storage."

Mrs. Withers walked to the stairs and slowly started up.

"I wonder what she's going to find out," Brandon whispered.

"I don't know," I said. *"I don't understand how she can know things without seeing them."*

"Well, you can smell flowers and know that there are flowers nearby, even if you don't see them," Brandon said.

He had a good point. Maybe being a medium or a psychic was like that. Maybe they just sort of 'sniffed out' ghosts.

While we waited, Mom and Dad talked quietly to one another, and I couldn't hear what they were saying. The only thing I could hear was Davis in his bedroom, making truck noises. Brandon flipped his model car over in his hand, back and forth.

And no sounds came from upstairs.

Finally, after what seemed like hours, Mrs. Withers came down the steps. Her face was stern, and she looked worried.

But, when she explained what was in our house, I wasn't worried.

I was *terrified*.

chapter nine

Mrs. Withers sat down on the couch, next to me.

"There is not a lot I can tell you," she said, "but there are some things I know for sure. First, you most certainly have a ghost in your home. Second, this ghost is very, very angry. I don't know why, but this ghost is mad. He wants something, and he is determined to get it."

Mom and Dad looked worried. "What does he want?" Dad asked.

"I'm not sure," Mrs. Withers said, shaking her head slowly. "It's not clear to me."

"Did you . . . did you *talk* to the ghost?" Mom asked.

Mrs. Withers shook her head. "No, no," she said. "It's not often that I talk to ghosts. But I can sense them, I can experience them. Sometimes, I can even know their thoughts."

All of this was really freaking me out. A real ghost? In our house? What would we do? Could we get rid of him?

"One thing that is strange," Mrs. Withers continued, "is that he is an old ghost. He's old, but he hasn't been in this home very long. Perhaps he was just a wandering spirit and took a liking to this home." She looked at Mom and Dad. "Tell me," she said, "before you bought this house, was it empty?"

Mom and Dad looked at each other.

"Yes," Dad said. "The people who owned the home moved out over a year ago. The house has been empty while it was for sale."

"Ah!" Mrs. Withers said. "I think what we have here is a wandering ghost who found a quiet place to haunt. However, when you moved in—"

"—it wasn't quiet anymore," Mom said.

"Exactly," Mrs. Withers said. "I think this ghost is angry because he thinks it's his home. You have disturbed him, and he wants you out."

"But . . . we just bought this place," Dad said. "We just moved in. We can't leave. This is *our* home now. We're not moving."

"Nor should you," Mrs. Withers said. She was smiling now. "But I wouldn't be too troubled. Ghosts rarely harm anyone and are usually more of a nuisance than anything. I think I can take care of this, but I'll need a few things. I'll be back in the morning, and we'll get rid of your ghost for good."

That made me feel better. Mrs. Withers was a bit odd, but she seemed to know what she was talking about. I was glad to hear her say that we could get rid of the ghost. I sure didn't want him appearing in the night, scaring the daylights out of us!

That night, when we went to bed, Mom and Dad decided that Davis would sleep in their room. They knew he would be freaked out totally if the ghost happened to appear and he saw it. I slept in my brothers' room on the bottom bunk, where Davis usually slept.

And I have to admit: I was a little scared about going to bed. True, Mrs. Withers said that ghosts normally don't hurt people, but I couldn't help being a little afraid.

Mom came into the room to say good night. She bent down and kissed me on the cheek. "Don't worry," she said. "Mrs. Withers will be back in the morning. She'll take care of our ghost."

"I hope so," I said.

"She will," Mom said. "I'm going to leave your door open. If anything happens, just holler."

Mom turned off the light as she left, but the night light in the hall provided plenty of light.

The words of Mrs. Withers drifted in my head. *Ghosts rarely harm anyone,* she'd said. I pulled the covers up to my chin. *Ghosts rarely harm anyone.*

Ghosts rarely harm anyone. I kept telling myself this over and over until I fell asleep.

It was a whimpering sound that awoke me sometime later. At first, I didn't know what it was . . . and then I realized it was my brother.

I opened my eyes . . . and was horrified to see the ghost standing in the middle of the bedroom! He was reaching toward me, looking right at me!

And he was speaking. He was saying something, and, like last night, his words were garbled and seemed far away, like he was talking in an tunnel. But I could make out enough to understand.

"I've come for the boy!" he said, shaking his fist at me. *"I've come . . . for . . . the . . . BOY!"*

I screamed, and screamed, and screamed.

I could hear loud noises coming from down the hall, and I knew Mom and Dad were on their way. Brandon was screaming just as loud as I was.

"I've come for the boy!" the ghost was still saying, but he was fading fast. By the time Mom and Dad got there and turned on the light, the ghost was only a murky white fog . . . and then he was gone.

"Did you see him?!?!" Brandon shrieked. "Did

you see him?!?!"

"Yes, we saw him," Dad said. "Are you guys okay?"

"Yeah," I said. I was trembling in the bed. "But the ghost said he was 'coming for the boy!' He was saying it over and over!"

"All right," Dad said. "Kirsten and Brandon . . . come with us. We'll all stay together for the rest of the night."

We scrambled out of bed and followed Mom down the hall and into their bedroom. Dad went into the garage and came back with two sleeping bags. He gave one to me and one to Brandon, and we rolled them out on the floor. Amazingly, Davis was still asleep on the bed. All of the commotion had failed to wake him.

"What if he comes back?" Brandon asked.

"We'll figure that out if it happens," Dad replied. "But remember: Mrs. Withers said that ghosts rarely harm anyone."

"But he was saying that he was coming for the boy," I said. "Which could only mean Brandon or

Davis."

"Everyone is safe in here," Mom said, trying to reassure us. But I could tell that she wasn't all that certain. I was sure that she was scared, too . . . at least a little bit. We all were. Only Dad seemed like he wasn't afraid. Maybe he wasn't; I couldn't tell. I was just glad that he wasn't out of town.

Mom was able to fall asleep, but Dad read for awhile. Brandon fell asleep in his sleeping bag, and Davis never once awoke.

For me, however, it wasn't that easy. I kept seeing the ghost in my mind, hearing his awful words over and over again. It was horrible. It seemed like hours before I was able to get back to sleep.

In the morning when I woke up, the bedroom was empty. Apparently, I'd slept a lot longer than anyone else, and when I looked at the clock on Mom and Dad's dresser, I saw that it was nearly 10 o'clock! I must've slept in because I'd had such a hard time falling back to sleep.

I crawled out of my sleeping bag, stood, and walked into the kitchen where Mom, Dad, Brandon, and Davis sat at the table, eating cereal.

"You're awake," Mom said as I sat down in a chair. She picked up the box of cereal and poured some in an empty bowl. A half gallon of milk sat on the table, and I picked it up and poured some over my cereal.

"I had a hard time getting back to sleep last night," I said. "I was really freaked out."

"I think we all were," Dad said, "except for Davis."

"When is Mrs. Withers going to be here?" I asked.

"Any time now," Mom answered, taking a sip of coffee.

"I hope it's soon," Brandon said. "I don't want to ever see that thing again."

"Mrs. Withers will see to that, I'm sure," Dad said.

I finished my cereal and helped Mom clean the kitchen. Just as I was drying the last bowl, the doorbell rang.

"She's here! She's here!" Brandon exclaimed,

and he raced for the front door and opened it. Mrs. Withers stood there, but she was looking up. Apparently, she was still worried about the spider she'd seen the day before.

"Hello, Mrs. Withers," Mom said as she walked to the front door. "Please . . . come in."

"Thank you," Mrs. Withers replied. She strode into the living room carrying a black leather bag.

Dad placed his cereal bowl in the sink and walked into the living room.

"Hi, Mrs. Withers," he said.

"Hello," Mrs. Withers replied. "Ready to take care of your ghost?" She seemed good-natured about the whole thing, and it seemed strange: here I was with three grown adults, and they were talking about getting rid of a ghost.

"I think we're more than ready," Dad said, and he and Mom explained what had happened last night.

"And he spoke to you?" Mrs. Withers asked me.

I nodded. "Yeah," I replied. "He said 'I've come for the boy', and he kept repeating it over and over."

Mrs. Withers seemed very puzzled by this.

"That's very strange," she said. "Ghosts aren't capable of taking someone. I don't know why he would say such a thing. Ghosts can, at times, take an object with them. Why, just last week, I visited a home in Pontiac where a ghost was taking things like umbrellas, dishes, utensils . . . things like that. But ghosts can't take a human being. It's just not possible."

"So, we weren't in any danger last night?" Mom asked.

"Well, I can't say for sure. But I can say that if a ghost says he's 'coming for the boy', he's probably just doing it to scare you. Ghosts will do that, sometimes." She held up her bag. "I can also say this: what I have in here will take care of your ghost once and for all."

Mrs. Withers unzipped the bag. I was really curious about what she had that was going to make the ghost go away. To my amazement, the only thing she pulled out was a white spray can with bold red letters.

"This is guaranteed to do the trick," she said, holding it up for us to see.

When I read the label, however, I couldn't believe it.

"Ghost-Be-Gone," Mom read out loud.

She has to be kidding! I thought. *There's actually a product called Ghost-Be-Gone?!?!* How incredibly silly. I'd never heard of such a thing. But, then again, why would I?

Mrs. Withers nodded. "It's the best product you can buy to get rid of pesky ghosts," she said. "Of course, they don't sell it to just anyone. You have to be licensed, like me."

"But how does it work?" I asked.

"Simple," Mrs. Withers replied. "In this can are a mix of special herbs and spices that ghosts simply can't stand. All I have to do is spray it around your house. If there is a ghost here, he's not going to like it, and he'll leave right away."

It seemed impossible. But, then again, Mrs. Withers was a professional. She knew what she was doing. And if all she had to do was go around the house with a spray can to get rid of our ghost, I was all for it.

Unfortunately for Mrs. Withers, and for us, things weren't going to go as she'd planned. In fact, her plan was about to backfire, and soon, we all were going to be in a lot of trouble.

chapter eleven

Mrs. Withers placed the black leather bag on the couch. "Now," she began, "I'll need you all to remain here while I work. You have a young one. Where is he?"

"Davis is in his room," Mom said.

"It would be best if you are all together," Mrs. Withers said. "Just in case anything goes wrong."

What could go wrong? I wondered. *Mrs. Withers*

makes it sound simple. She'll walk around the house, spray her can of Ghost-Be-Gone, and poof! The ghost will be gone.

"Davis!" Mom called out. "Come here, please!"

Davis came out of his room. His hair was pointing in all different directions, like he'd just gotten out of bed. Maybe he had. He looked funny. "What?" he said.

"Come in here for a little while," Mom said. "Mrs. Withers is going to do a little . . . housecleaning . . . for us."

Davis trundled into the living room and sat on the floor. He watched Mrs. Withers like a dog watches a bird at the feeder. I didn't think he was really aware of what had been going on, and Mom and Dad wanted to keep it that way. They thought he would be too scared by the fact that there was a real ghost living in our house.

But all of that would be over, soon. Mrs. Withers would see to that.

"All right," Mrs. Withers said, "I'm ready to begin. This shouldn't take long at all." And with that,

Mrs. Withers raised the can of Ghost-Be-Gone and held it out. She pumped the spray top a couple of times. Each time she did this, a fine, gray mist shot out. It evaporated almost instantly.

"It's like Mom spraying air freshener around the house," I whispered to Brandon.

"Yeah," he replied. *"Except Mom's air freshener doesn't get rid of ghosts."*

Mrs. Withers moved to each corner of the living room. We watched her intently, except for Davis, who became bored and was now pretending to draw pictures on the wood floor with his fingers.

"It won't be long," Mrs. Withers was saying as she sprayed the Ghost-Be-Gone around the living room. "I just need to make sure that I spray every room of your home."

After she finished spraying the living room, Mrs. Withers slowly made her way down the hall. Every few steps she would pause and spray, then she would continue on. She vanished into my bedroom, then emerged a few moments later. Then, she moved on into Brandon and Davis's room, then into the bathroom, and then into Mom and Dad's room.

"Won't be long now," we heard her say. "This ghost will be good as gone."

When she finished in Mom and Dad's room, she returned to the living room. She headed up the stairs, pausing every few steps to spray the Ghost-Be-Gone. We could hear her spraying Dad's office and the storage room upstairs. Then, she came back down.

"Do you have a basement?" she asked.

Dad pointed to a door on the other side of the kitchen. "Right over there, through that door," Dad said. "It's still filled with a lot of unpacked boxes and crates, though."

"That doesn't matter," Mrs. Withers said. "I'll just be a minute." She walked through the kitchen and opened the basement door, pausing for just a moment to spray the Ghost-Be-Gone. Then, she vanished down the steps.

Suddenly, there was a loud clicking sound at the front door . . . the sound of a lock being turned. All of us jumped—even Mom and Dad. Dad got up and went to the front door. He tried the doorknob, but it wouldn't turn. He tried turning the bolt lock, but it wouldn't turn, either. Still holding the knob, he shook the door, trying to open it.

"It's locked," he said. "It locked all by itself."

There was another sound at the door that leads into our garage. Dad hurried through the living room to the door, only to find it locked. He tugged on the door, but it wouldn't open.

I was starting to get scared. What was going on? What was happening?

Then, all the window shutters began slamming shut. They made a terrible racket. Davis placed his hands over his ears. Mom leapt to her feet. My eyes darted around the room. In seconds, we were in a murky darkness. Then—

Silence.

My heart was hammering in my chest.

"Wha . . . wha . . . what's . . . hap . . . happening?" Brandon stammered. He, too, was frightened . . . and for good reason.

"I don't know," Mom said. Dad rushed into the living room. "The door to the garage is locked, and so is the back door!" he said.

Mrs. Withers suddenly appeared at the top of the basement steps. She looked horrified.

"Something is wrong!" she exclaimed. Just as she uttered those words, a lamp in the living room rose into the air, all by itself! It was sent flying across the room like it had been thrown by an invisible hand! The lamp shattered against the wall, and broken fragments tumbled to the floor.

Dad tried the front door. "It's still locked!" he said. He slid open a window and banged on the closed shutters. "I . . . I don't understand!" he said. "There aren't any locks on the shutters, but I can't get them to open!"

I felt a wave of cold horror wash over me as I suddenly realized we were trapped in our home . . . with a very, very angry ghost.

chapter twelve

12

More things began flying around the house, all by themselves. Plates spun in the air and whirled around like flying saucers, finally slamming into the wall and exploding into dozens of pieces that fell to the floor with sharp tinkling sounds.

"Get down!" Dad ordered. Brandon and I dropped to the floor. Even Mrs. Withers seemed frightened and confused. She, too, fell to the floor so she wouldn't get hit by any flying objects. Mom scooped up Davis, who was fascinated by the bizarre activities throughout the house. It didn't seem to scare him one bit! He seemed amused that things were flying around the room like toys.

"Is everyone all right?" Dad called out. He was now kneeling in the kitchen and had to duck to miss the toaster, which was spinning in the air above him.

"We're okay," Mom said.

Brandon was in a panic. "Make them stop, Dad!" he exclaimed.

Dad reached up and plucked the phone from the wall. He pushed the speaker button, and we could hear a dial tone . . . then three sharp beeps as he dialed 9-1-1. Then, we heard a ring and a click. But it wasn't answered by the 9-1-1 operator. Instead, a haunting, deep voice growled: *"Don't bother calling for help! This line is DEAD!"* It was followed by evil laughter and a loud click as the connection was cut. Dad tried to dial other numbers, but none of them worked.

Meanwhile, things were still flying around the room. I had to duck several times so I wouldn't get hit by a flying bowl or a glass or a picture frame. There were broken pieces of things all over the floor. It was awful. Most of this, however, was taking place in the living room. Dad was still in the kitchen, on the floor, and he ordered all of us to crawl over to him. I started out first, followed by Brandon, then Mom and Davis, and Mrs. Withers. When we were all gathered in the kitchen, most of the things that had been flying about the house had stopped. The only thing we could hear was our own heavy breathing.

"Maybe the ghost is gone," I said.

Mrs. Withers shook her head. "No, he's still here," she said. "I can feel him."

"But you said the Ghost-Be-Gone would make him leave," Mom said.

"It's always worked before," Mrs. Withers replied. "I've never had anything like this happen before."

"What are we going to do?" Brandon asked. He sounded like he was about to cry. "We're trapped in our own home!"

"There's got to be a way out," Dad said. "We

just have to think."

Suddenly, there was a faint scraping noise behind me. I turned.

Something moved on the refrigerator! It was one of my magnets! The letter G was moving all by itself! While we watched, other letters began to move.

"They're forming words all by themselves!" I said.

Mrs. Withers shook her head. "No, not all by themselves," she said. "The ghost is doing it. The ghost is trying to communicate with us!"

Finally, the letters stopped moving . . . and the words they spelled out were horrifying.

give me
what is
m ine

chapter thirteen

The words spelled out:

GIVE ME WHAT IS MINE

Dad read the sentence out loud, and so did Mrs. Withers.

"What does that mean?" I asked. "What's his?"

Mrs. Withers looked at me. "Didn't you say the ghost tried to talk to you last night?" she asked.

I nodded. "Yeah," I replied. "He was saying

something like 'I've come for the boy' over and over."

"But that doesn't make sense," Mom said. "Brandon and Davis are the only boys here. Why would he want one of them?"

"I'm not going anywhere with any ghost," Brandon said, shaking his head.

"Me neither," Davis said, but I don't think he really knew what we were talking about. Now that objects weren't flying all over the house, he'd become bored again.

Mrs. Withers truly looked perplexed. "I don't know what's going on here," she said. "But I don't think we're in danger."

"Unless we get hit by something flying around the room," I said.

Mrs. Withers nodded. "Yes, you're right . . . but I don't think this ghost is intent on harming anyone. Clearly, he wants something."

I looked at the refrigerator magnets and read the sentence in my mind. *Give me what is mine. Give me what is mine.*

"Maybe he thinks the house is his, and we took

it from him," Mom said.

Again, Mrs. Withers shook her head. "Often, ghosts and humans live in harmony with one another. I find many homes inhabited by ghosts, and the owners never know about it. It's possible that your previous home had ghosts, but you were unaware. Most ghosts don't cause trouble. Only when something disturbs them will they cause a fuss. And the ghost in this house is definitely causing a fuss."

I looked around the kitchen floor and peered into the living room. For a ghost that didn't want to hurt us, he sure was making an awful mess.

"Is there any other way out of the house?" Mrs. Withers asked.

"No," Dad said, shaking his head. "I'm afraid we're—"

He stopped speaking suddenly. "Wait a minute!" he said. "There's a window near the ceiling in the basement! It's the only window of the house that doesn't have shutters! Maybe we can get out that way!"

Dad stood and nervously looked around, not

wanting some object to come flying off the counter and bonk him in the head. "You guys stay here," Dad ordered. "I'll go check it out."

"Be careful," Mom said.

As it turned out, however, Dad didn't get very far. He opened the basement door . . . *and was face-to-face with the old ghost!*

Dad was so startled he nearly fell when he leapt backward. The rest of us crawled to the far side of the kitchen to put as much distance as possible between us and the ghost.

At the top of the basement stairs, the ghost glared at Dad. He raised his arm and pointed. He began talking, but, again, it was really difficult to understand what he was saying.

Brandon spoke. "Why is he so hard to—"

"Shhhhh," Mrs. Withers said softly. "Let's listen."

The old man seemed to be repeating what he'd said the night before, that he had 'come for the boy'. It was creeping me out. Even Davis, who hadn't paid much attention to all that was going on, was scared.

He'd started to cry, and he was hugging Mom tightly. "I want my truck," he sniffled. Usually, when he was upset, he'd have his truck under his arm. Some kids have blankets . . . my brother has an old wooden truck.

The old ghost's voice grew louder and more sinister . . . and I suddenly realized what he was saying! I gasped.

"That's it!" I exclaimed. "I think I know what he's really saying!"

chapter fourteen

Everyone looked at me, but they kept glancing back at the ghost.

"What?" Dad asked. "What do you think he's saying?"

"He's not saying he's come for the *boy*," I said. "He's saying that he's come for his *toy!*"

"That doesn't make sense, either," Brandon said. "What toy?"

My mind raced as I began to put two-and-two together. "Mrs. Withers," I asked, "is it possible that this ghost isn't from this house?"

Mrs. Withers glanced at the ghost, who was now beginning to fade. He was dissipating into the air, just like he had done before. In seconds, he was gone completely.

"Well, yes, it's possible," she replied. "Usually, though, ghosts like to haunt one place. They don't travel around very often."

"Is it possible that the ghost followed us from our old home?" I asked.

Mom and Dad looked at me like I was crazy. So did Brandon.

"Yes," Mrs. Withers said, "that is also possible."

"But we didn't have a ghost in our old home," Mom said.

"We don't know that for sure," I replied. "Like Mrs. Withers said: ghosts and people can live together in the same house, and the people never know the ghosts are there. What if this ghost followed us from our old home because he wants something that's his?"

"That could be," Mrs. Withers said. "But what toy does he want?"

"The only toy we brought with us from our old home!" I said. "Davis's old wooden truck! I'll bet it belongs to the ghost!"

"That might be it!" Mrs. Withers exclaimed. Her eyes lit up. "Quickly! Can you bring me the truck?"

"Davis," Dad said, "where is your truck? Is it in your room?"

Davis nodded silently.

"I'll go get it," Dad said. He stood, rushed down the hall, and returned a moment later carrying Davis's truck. He handed it to Mrs. Withers, who carefully took it in both hands.

She closed her eyes while she cradled the truck before her.

"Yes, yes," she said softly. "There's something here. A great amount of energy. There's—"

All of a sudden, Mrs. Withers' whole body seemed to go stiff. She let out a gasp and then was silent for a long time. We all watched, not wanting to say anything, not wanting to disturb her. Finally, after a few minutes had passed, Mrs. Withers opened her eyes. She looked . . . different, somehow. Confident and sure of herself. She smiled thinly.

"I now know what has occurred," she said. "I don't have all the answers, but Kirsten, you're right. This toy *did* come from your old home. It actually belonged to the ghost, a long time ago, when he was a boy growing up in that same house. My guess is that the ghost is very attached to this truck. Perhaps it was special because it was his only toy as a child. Or maybe someone special made it for him, like his father. Regardless, it is his toy . . . and he wants it back. Only then will he go away."

"But, if he wanted it, why didn't he just *take* it?" Dad asked.

"He can't," Mrs. Withers said. "He is a ghost, and his energy isn't as strong as the energy of a human being. There is an energy that is blocking his, an energy stronger. Someone has formed a bond with the truck. Someone has become very fond of the toy. Until that person agrees to release the truck, the ghost will forever continue to want it back."

"You mean . . . you mean Davis has to give the toy to the ghost?" I asked.

"Not necessarily," Mrs. Withers said. "What he will need to do is to give it up in his mind."

Mom frowned curiously. "In his mind?" she said. "How does he do that?"

"Simple," Mrs. Withers said. "You see, I'll bet that Davis loves his truck. Is that correct?"

I nodded. "He takes it with him everywhere."

Mrs. Withers continued. "All your brother needs to do is realize that the truck is far more important to this old ghost than it is to him. If he could do that, he would lessen his 'energy hold' on the truck. In essence, he needs to 'give up' the truck and allow the old ghost to have it." Everyone was now looking at Brandon.

"Do you understand what Mrs. Withers is saying?" Dad asked.

Davis bobbed his head.

"Will you give up your truck?" Mom asked.

Davis hesitated, but he nodded. "Yeah," he peeped.

"Good," Mrs. Withers said. "First thing: I think

it's safe for us all to stand."

I'd been so caught up in what was going on that I forgot we were all still seated on the floor. We got to our feet.

Mrs. Withers handed the truck to Davis. "What I need you to do is to think about something else that's important to you. Something more important than your truck."

Davis thought about this for a moment. "A new truck?" he asked.

Mrs. Withers nodded. "That's fine. Think about a new truck. A *better* truck than you now have."

"In fact," Dad said, "we can go to the toy store and get you a brand new one later today. How's that?"

Davis's eyes lit up. He always loved going to the toy store. Now that he knew he was getting a new truck, he was really excited.

"If I'm gettin' a new truck, I don't need this one," he said, holding the truck out and looking at it.

Suddenly, an amazing thing happened . . . .

chapter fifteen

15

The truck rose into the air all by itself! We all stared in amazement as the old wooden toy floated up, drifting over our heads. It moved gently, as if it were being carried. No one said a word as the truck drifted into the living room and hovered near the ceiling, above the coffee table.

"What's happening?" Dad asked quietly.

"The ghost is taking possession of the truck,"

Mrs. Withers replied. "Watch."

Soon, a fine mist began to appear in the living room. At first, it looked like smoke, drifting like a snake. Then, a form began to take shape, growing in brightness and density.

"It's him!" Brandon hissed. *"It's the ghost! He's appearing!"*

Brandon was right! The ghost was taking shape right before our eyes! I could make out his legs and arms. Then, I could see his face. He wasn't looking at us, but, rather, at the truck that was floating in the air. We watched as the ghost slowly reached out and took the truck in his hands. He held it out for a moment. Then, he turned . . . and looked at Brandon. The ghost didn't say anything, but you could tell by his face that he was grateful.

Then, just as he had before, the ghost began to vanish . . . along with the truck. He faded into a cloudy mist and, after a few moments, disappeared completely.

Mrs. Withers smiled. "I think that's the end of your haunting," she said. "I don't think you'll have any more ghosts to worry about."

"That was the freakiest thing I've ever seen," Brandon said.

"Me, too," Dad agreed. "I hope we don't have to go through something like this again."

We thanked Mrs. Withers and said good-bye. She left, saying that if we ever needed help again, she would be happy to come back.

"Thanks," Mom said, "but I hope we never have to call you again."

Later that day, Dad took Davis to the toy store, where he bought him a shiny, new yellow and red truck, made of metal. Davis spent the rest of the day in the sandbox in the backyard, playing with it. To this day, it's his favorite truck.

And thankfully, Mrs. Withers was right. To this day, we don't have any trouble with ghosts. I've told some of my new friends what happened to us, but most of them don't believe me. That's okay. I know the truth, and so does my family.

Still, sometimes as I walk through our home, I catch a glimpse of something that seems to move.

Sometimes, I'll hear noises in the night, and wonder:

Is there a ghost here, living in this house, like there had been at our old home? Is he or she with us right now, in our home, living here with us?

Maybe, maybe not. I guess it really doesn't matter, as long as we're all happy . . . including the ghosts.

THE END